This book belongs to:

_____

_____

_____

First published by Walker Books Ltd.,
87 Vauxhall Walk, London SE11 5HJ

Copyright © 2014 by Lucy Cousins
Lucy Cousins font copyright © 2014 by Lucy Cousins
Illustrated in the style of Lucy Cousins by King Rollo Films Ltd.

Maisy™. Maisy is a registered trademark of Walker Books Ltd., London.

First U.S. edition 2014

Library of Congress Catalog Card Number 2013943077
ISBN 978-0-7636-6950-8 (hardcover)
ISBN 978-0-7636-7237-9 (paperback)

13 14 15 16 17 18 CCP 10 9 8 7 6 5 4 3 2 1

Printed in Shenzhen, Guangdong, China

This book was typeset in Lucy Cousins.
The illustrations were done in gouache.

Candlewick Press
99 Dover Street
Somerville, Massachusetts 02144

visit us at www.candlewick.com

Maisy Goes to the Movies

Lucy Cousins

CANDLEWICK PRESS

Today, Maisy and her friends
are going to the movies.
"Oh, I am **SO** excited!" says Tallulah.
"Can we buy popcorn?" asks Charley.
"I **LOVE** popcorn!"

There are lots of different movies showing. Which one will they decide to see?

Dusty Cowboy

HERO IN THE JUNGLE

SAM, THE HAPPY SHARK

A Royal Romance

Maisy buys five tickets for "Hero in the Jungle" and some SNACKS!

Popcorn, juice,
and ice cream—
YUM!

Maisy and her friends like adventure
movies, and Troy T. Tiger (a very BIG
movie star) is starring
in this one.

Wow! It's a BIG screen! Tallulah wants to sit in the middle, and Cyril wants to sit next to Maisy.

Eddie and Charley want to sit at the very front!

The lights come down slowly, and the movie begins.

Cyril doesn't like the dark theater. "Don't worry, Cyril," says Maisy. "You can hold my hand."

"That's my favorite movie star!"
cries Eddie when Troy T. Tiger
appears on the screen.

Everybody in the theater says,
"Shhhhhh!" and "Quiet!"

Charley laughs so much that he knocks some popcorn on the floor. Oops!

It's nearly halfway through the movie now, and Tallulah needs to go to the bathroom.

"Me too," says Cyril.

"Me three!" says Eddie.

So they go as fast as they can.

And wash their hands very quickly.

"Hurry! Hurry!" says Eddie. They don't want to miss anything.

There's one very scary part
when Troy T. Tiger meets a
big, huge . . . DINOSAUR!

"I can't watch!" says Cyril,
and he hides behind his hands.

Afterward, Maisy and her friends talk about their favorite parts of the movie.

"What shall we do now?" asks Cyril.
"I know," says
Eddie. . . .

"Let's go see the movie again!"

HERO IN THE JUNGLE